For Charlotte, my Velveteen Kitty. Forever and for always.

Text and illustrations copyright © 2014 by Ashley Spires

Published in Canada by Tundra Books, a division of Random House of Canada Limited,
One Toronto Street, Suite 300, Toronto, Ontario M5C 2V6

Published in the United States by Tundra Books of Northern New York,
P.O. Box 1030, Plattsburgh, New York 12901

Library of Congress Control Number: 2013953676

Library and Archives Canada Cataloguing in Publication

Spires, Ashley, 1978–, author, illustrator
        Edie's ensembles / written and illustrated by Ashley Spires.

Issued in print and electronic formats.
ISBN 978-1-77049-490-9 (bound).—ISBN 978-1-77049-491-6 (epub)

        I. Title.

PS8637.P57E35 2014   jC813'.6   C2013-906913-5
                                                               C2013-906914-3

Edited by Tara Walker
Designed by Kelly Hill

The artwork in this book was rendered digitally and with a great deal of retail "research."
The text was set in Neutraface.
www.tundrabooks.com

Printed and bound in China

1 2 3 4 5 6   19 18 17 16 15 14

Edie's Ensembles

written and illustrated by

Ashley Spires

Tundra Books

Edie wore the most marvelous clothes. Pants, skirts, jackets and shoes. Sweaters, dresses, hats and scarves. She had them in every color, and she loved wearing them.

The hall at school was her runway. Each day Edie showed off her finest outfits.
She was known for her great taste and stylish flair.

Andrew was Edie's best friend.

They spent a *lot* of time playing dress-up.
Some outfits worked, some didn't, but
their favorites always made it to school
the next day.

One morning Edie arrived in one of her best ensembles. But as she strolled into school, she heard no whispers of admiration. In class no one noticed the swish of her silk scarf.

And at recess no one mentioned her Italian suede shoes. After lunch someone *finally* said something about her turquoise cashmere sweater . . .

But it was just to tell her there was mustard on it.

The walk home with Andrew was a quiet one. No one noticed her clothes that day. No one paid her any attention.

Edie decided that they needed to hold an emergency dress-up session.

Tomorrow her outfit *had* to be an eye-catching show-stopper.

And it was! The next day *everyone* noticed Edie. Even mean Kyle said something. Sure, it was just to ask if she owned a mirror, but the point was, he *noticed* her.

Edie felt so good getting all that attention that on the way home she started to plan the next day's outfit. She was going to have to think up an even more terrific ensemble for tomorrow.

It took some time. Quite a long time actually. But she managed to find something that would knock everyone's socks off.

The next day brought Edie more compliments and attention. She was talking to kids she had never even met before. Her clothes were making her popular! Edie felt *amazing*.

Nice hat!

Great colors!

Edie wanted to make each ensemble better than the last, so she and Andrew spent all their time planning outfits. Even Andrew thought he might try a new look.

But Edie didn't think that was a good idea.

No.

As time went by, all of Edie's clothes started to look dull to her. So she decided to change things up.

She ripped her old shirts and dresses apart, sewing them into exciting new creations.

Sometimes she even added other things, just to make it interesting. Making new clothes took all of Edie's time and attention.

At school the comments started to change too.
But Edie didn't mind, as long as everyone still talked about her.

Some of her outfits were hard to wear. Most of the time she couldn't see or hear or move very well.

But Edie was still getting lots of attention.

She's bonkers.

And then, one morning when
she was running late . . .

Edie got stuck.

Somebody was sure to notice, right?

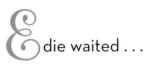

$\mathcal{E}$die waited . . .

and waited . . .

and waited.

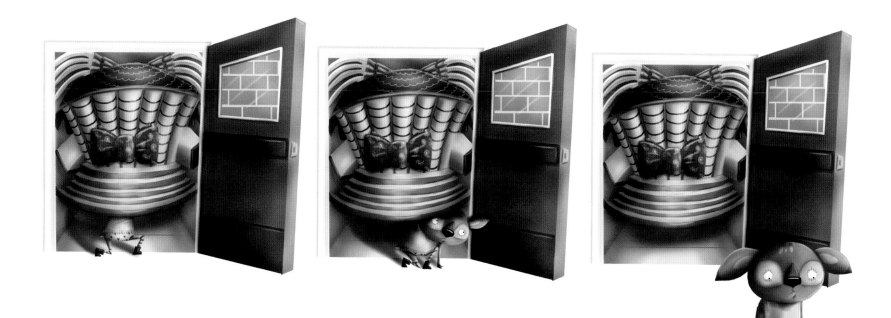

But no one came.

No one noticed she wasn't in class.

Not even Andrew.

As Edie trudged along, she wondered how she had become so alone.

When she arrived home, she walked right past her closet . . .

and looked at herself in the mirror.

She couldn't remember the last time she saw her arms,
her legs, her face or any other part of her. Edie had been
lost underneath all those clothes.

The next day she went to school in one of her most daring outfits. No one noticed Edie's ensemble.

But Calvin shared his carrots at recess . . .

and Deidre complimented her drawing
in art class . . .

and Jared and Kyle laughed at her jokes.

After school Edie found Andrew.

She told him how much she liked his outfit,
though she thought something was missing.

He completely agreed.

The End